FOLLOW THE BROOK

DOROTHY P. LATHROP

THE MACMILLAN COMPANY

NEW YORK

Books by Dorothy P. Lathrop

An Angel in the Woods

Bouncing Betsy

The Colt from Moon Mountain

Follow the Brook

Let Them Live

The Littlest Mouse

Puffy and the Seven Leaf Clover

Puppies for Keeps

Skittle Skattle Monkey

Who Goes There?

© DOROTHY P. LATHROP 1960

Library of Congress catalog card number:
60–13964

The Macmillan Company, New York
Brett-Macmillan Ltd., Galt, Ontario

PRINTED IN THE UNITED STATES OF AMERICA

To
Wendy and Judy
and
Vicky

FOLLOW THE BROOK

Taffy and Tansy crowded close to the wire window of their cage and watched the boys walk down the path and away. The two raccoons did not want to be left. They wanted to play.

Tansy called to them. Almost always when she made that soft, purring noise they would come back to see what she wanted. But now they hurried on, talking together as if they had not heard.

The raccoons, their cheeks pressed flat against the wire, tried hard to see around the curve of the path. Their ears were pointed toward the last faint sound of voices, but the chirping of a bird nearby was far louder. Soon they could hear only the soft rubbing of their own little black fingers across the wire. They were all alone in their cage at the edge of the woods.

Taffy and Tansy had lived in that cage as long as they could remember. At first it had been big enough to run in, but it was growing smaller and smaller until now one of them could hardly squeeze by the other. And there was no room at all to play.

Taffy climbed down to see what the boys had brought them to eat. But his sister pushed her small hand through the wire and tried to catch the leaves as they swung near on the breeze. She could not reach them. More than anything she wanted to get out to touch and to taste what now she could only see.

Often her quick fingers had snatched little moths right out of the air as they fluttered by. So when a dragonfly, its wings a blur, suddenly hung motionless before her eyes, her hand shot toward it. But she felt it dart between her outspread fingers.

Restlessly she felt for her only plaything, the padlock that fastened the door of the cage. It swung back and forth and rattled when she touched it. Now, because she could not catch the dragonfly, she pushed it so hard it swung wildly and clattered more loudly than ever before. Suddenly it was gone! She felt all around as far as her fingers could reach. It was nowhere.

Already Taffy had eaten more than his share of the dinner. He was picking up the last graham cracker! And they were a

special treat! Tansy scrambled down and tried to take it away from him. She was too late. He was dipping it into their drinking water. Perhaps he wanted to wash it, perhaps to soften it. Anyway it was softening nicely! He rubbed it between his palms, then tried to lift it out of the water. Where was it? Tansy helped him search, but though their four little hands groped way to the bottom of the crock, they could find no cracker.

They dabbled and splashed. It was fun to play in water! Then Taffy took hold of the crock and tipped it over and the water ran across the floor in a stream. They hurried after it, patting their hands in it until it all ran away and there was no more to play in. There was none to dip their food into either, and they had to eat it dry. Tansy was very thirsty. She put her nose way into the crock, but there was not a drop left. She put it in again and again, but still there was no water. She would have to wait until supper, but they had not thought of that when Taffy turned over the crock. Everyday they spilled the water after dinner and after supper too. There was never enough.

The two moved restlessly about the cage, back and forth, back and forth. Tansy watched Taffy's black-ringed tail trailing behind him. It brushed her as it passed, and suddenly she seized it in her jaws. Quickly he swung around and, grabbing

her by the scruff, shook her so hard she let go of his tail. Both growled as fiercely as if they were fighting, and the play got rougher and rougher. They rolled around together in one big furry ball, and Taffy bit Tansy's ear until she squealed. Sometimes when they played with the boys as roughly as with each other, the boys squealed too. They banged into walls and bounced off, but when they fell against the door, it began to open.

Instantly they stopped playing and thrust their noses through the crack, then their heads and then, because there was no one to push them back, their whole bodies. They stepped out into the woods. There on the ground lay the padlock. And because she had played with it so often, Tansy picked it up and carried it with her. But there were newer and more exciting things to see and touch and she soon dropped it. She wanted to see everything. Taffy had already disappeared behind the big rock they saw from the cage. She hurried after him. They would explore the whole woods!

The ground felt queer under their feet, not smooth like the floor of the cage. On it were dry sticks to be climbed over, stones that were rough and hard and hurt their feet, and little bushes that stood in the way. Tansy stopped to touch the leaves as she pushed by them. She walked with her head to the ground,

sniffing at everything. But Taffy lifted a quivering nose to catch a strange fresh smell in the air like that of the rain which sometimes fell outside their cage window. He hurried toward it. Could it be water?

He ran down a rocky slope and right into the brook without stopping. Just as hastily he backed out again, for the water was deeper than any ever spilled out of the crock. And it was running so fast it would be gone in a minute! He must be quick if he wanted to play in it. Tansy splashed in behind him.

Side by side they stood in the shallow water and groped over the bottom of the brook. They were not sure what they were hunting for, but they turned over stones and felt underneath them. They thrust their hands deep into the mud, but no living thing moved under their fingers. And all the while they gazed far away across the brook as if their eyes did not care what their hands were doing. Still the water ran on. Only a very big crock could have spilled so much water!

The raccoons were too curious about this exciting new world to stay long in one place. But since they could not bear to leave all that lovely water, they waded their way up the brook. They did not go very fast. There were too many things to look at. And when Taffy saw something hop out of sight behind a big rock, he stopped, climbed up and peered over the top. He

saw nothing, for the rabbit did not wait to be stared at by a creature so much bigger than he. The red squirrel was much bolder. He ran so far down a branch that his nose almost touched Tansy's, and he tried to shout her right out of his woods. He was so small and his barks so big that they nearly jounced him off the branch. Tansy soon lost interest in him and went on her way, but he followed her from tree to tree with his scolding.

The boys were a long way from the brook by now. All at once Bill began to walk slowly. And he looked worried.

"Davy, did you lock the cage?" he asked his little brother.

"No, why? Didn't *you*? You always do. Bill, *didn't* you?"

"I–don't–know. Can you remember hearing the lock click?"

Davy shook his head miserably.

"But the coons will get out!" he cried. "We've got to go back. Bill, Bill, hurry!"

Almost running, they started back home.

At that moment Tansy was lolling on a soft, mossy spot on the bank of the brook. The sun was warm on her fur, and it was pleasant to lie there after wading in the cold water. The sun almost never shone into the cage or made a spot on the floor big

enough to sit in. There was so much of everything here out of doors—so much water, so much sun, so many things to see. Tansy's small, black eyes followed the little birds as they darted in and out among the highest leaves, and her ears twitched at each sudden, joyous song. She watched the butterflies fluttering far out of her reach, and Taffy turning over stone after stone, hunting for something, anything to eat. And a chipmunk watched *her*. She lay so still that he dared to creep nearer to find out what she was, then took fright and dashed chittering into the ground.

Taffy began to wander up the brook again without even looking back to see whether his sister was coming. She was hustling down the bank, for she did not want to be left behind. And she galloped and splashed along after him.

They made their way slowly, stopping to dabble in each new part of the brook. But always they went on again, for who knew what they might find around each new turning?

"Ker-chug. Chug-chug-chug."

"Ker-chug-chug."

"CHUG! CHUG!"

The deep croaking came from just around the next bend. It sounded as if a lot of creatures were talking together. How big they must be to have such loud gruff voices!

16

The raccoons crept on very quietly and cautiously until they could peer around the corner. They saw no big animals—none even as big as themselves. But now there were no voices. Only the soft whispering and gurgling of water broke the silence.

Here the brook had widened into a pool and their feet sank into soft mud at its edges. Something wriggled under Tansy's foot. She reached down hastily and scooped it up, then scrambled up on a rock to look at her prize. It was a crawfish! She had found something at last! Holding it very tightly in both hands, she washed it carefully in the brook before she ate it.

The frogs stared at Taffy with unblinking, round eyes, and he looked right at the frogs but did not see them, for they were as motionless as the rocks they sat on. Only their throats moved with their breathing.

Taffy reached over the log toward the water. Perhaps he too could find a crawfish. Suddenly a piece of green moss leaped almost from under his hands. Too late he saw that it was alive! He lunged toward it. But the frog, with a farewell kick of its long, hind legs, plunged into the far side of the pool with a splash. And Taffy fell headfirst into the water!

The splash that Taffy made was much louder than the frog's. It sent little waves dancing to the edge of the pool. And when he came up, he was no longer interested in frogs. Two

muskrats were in the pool with him. They were swimming right at him, and they looked almost big enough to eat *him!* He climbed hastily up on the nearest rock out of their reach. He had never been wet all over before. No water in his cage had been this deep. He shook himself so hard that he even spattered Tansy.

The boys were all out of breath when they reached the cage at last.

"The door is open," said Bill.

"And the coons are gone!" cried Davy, his head in the cage.

"Where is the lock?" asked Bill. "Who took it away?"

"Taffy! Tansy!" called Davy, and listened.

"TAFFY! TANSY!" shouted Bill, but no little sharp noses were thrust out from behind rock or bush in answer.

"Perhaps those aren't really their names," said Davy. "It's just what *we* called them."

"They never did seem to know them—not like a dog does," agreed Bill.

"We'll have to find them. They'll get lost in the woods and there won't be anybody to feed them!"

"Maybe they're down by the brook. They love water."

And the boys, too, hurried off to the brook.

20

Taffy and Tansy had wandered too far away to hear them call. They could not bear to stay long in one place, now that they need not walk back and forth between walls all day long. Now they could go wherever they wished. They went on and on up the brook for best of all they loved to feel the cold, fresh water swirl around their legs and run between their fingers. It made Taffy so happy that he grabbed Tansy by the tail, and they tussled and scuffled and hopped up in the air and tumbled back again into the water. Soon both were nearly as wet as Taffy after he had fallen into the frogs' deep pool.

Tired at last of playing, they climbed up into the woods and lay on the dry leaves to rest. They rolled on the warm, sweet pine needles until their thick fur, musty from living too long in the cage, began to smell clean and spicy like the needles. Content, they no longer felt restless. They lifted their noses and sniffed the cool earthy fragrance of the woods and almost remembered that they had once lived here when they were very little before they were taken away and shut up in a cage.

The boys stood uncertainly by the brook.

"Do you suppose they would go *up* the brook or *down?*" asked Bill. But Davy only shook his head, for he did not know.

"I'll go down and you go up, Davy. And holler if you see

them." And Bill and Davy started off in opposite directions.

Soon neither could hear the other's footsteps. And if they heard a rustling in the fallen leaves, it was never a raccoon who made it, but only a towhee hopping and scratching for bugs or a chipmunk scurrying back to his hole.

"Bill! Bill!" It was so faint a call that Bill hardly heard it. He raced toward it. Had Davy found them? No, he was only pointing down at some little footprints in the mud.

"Look, Bill, they went *this* way—*up* the brook."

And the boys followed the way the footprints pointed.

Far away as they were, Taffy and Tansy, too, heard that call. They stood up high on their hind legs and looked down the brook. They listened intently. Then Taffy turned and ran. He doubled his legs under him and ran so fast Tansy could hardly keep up. They were not running back to the boys. They were running away.

At last they felt safe again, but they were getting very hungry. It had been a long time since dinner. There must be more crawfish and frogs in the water. Their fingers felt busily for them while their little eyes peered sharply out of their black masks and kept watch down the brook.

But they did not keep watch overhead. Suddenly a big, blue

bird dived out of the sky and into the water with an enormous splash! The poor raccoons shrank back and arched their backs in fright, and their fur stood out all over. And just as suddenly the kingfisher rose out of the water and flew away with a wriggling fish in his long, sharp bill. His noisy rattling laugh laid their ears back on their heads.

Taffy and Tansy looked after him in wonder. Where had he found that fish? Not one had come swimming within reach of their hands. *They* had not caught even a frog, but only a few crawfish, some black beetles and a snail and they were growing hungrier and hungrier. Taffy had almost caught a little snake, but its tail slipped through his fingers as it wriggled between some stones.

The boys sat down to rest. Their legs were tired from climbing over so many rocks.

"Perhaps we'll never find them," mourned Davy. "Perhaps they're lost and can't find their way home."

"Maybe they don't *want* to come back," said Bill.

"But I thought they liked us!" cried Davy. "They play with us, and we give them good things to eat, and everything."

"I guess they liked us a little," said Bill. "But we were all they had to like.

"Come on," he said, getting up. "Maybe we'll find them yet. Maybe they're not very far away."

Neither boy guessed how near they were! For just around the next bend the two raccoons were standing very straight and still and listening. Then Taffy turned and dashed into the woods just before the boys came into sight.

It was too late for Tansy to follow him. Where could she hide? A hollow stump stood by the side of the brook, its dead roots in the water. Quickly Tansy dived between them and, squeezing up into its empty trunk, was out of sight in no time.

There she clung with her sharp little claws, not making a move, not making a sound until the boys had gone on up the brook. Then very cautiously she peered over the top of the stump.

Where was Taffy? She crept out of her hiding place and looked all around but could not see him. She was all alone. Was that the boys' voices again? Were they coming back? She retreated toward the stump and stood listening. But it was only the brook whispering and talking to itself as it ran past her.

Still Taffy did not come. Then she gave that little purring call that had always made the boys come back and rub her ears and ask what she wanted. Soft as it was, Taffy must have heard,

28

for, very slowly, looking all around him, he came out of the woods.

And side by side, their bodies low to the ground, they ran stealthily back *down* the brook. Often they stopped to look back and listen. But birds were singing in the trees, squirrels leaping from branch to branch and chipmunks whisking among the fallen leaves, and not one of them was warning the others of danger. Soon the raccoons too began to feel safe once more.

Tansy put her arms around a tree and looked up at the branches so far above her. How she would like to be up there! She had never climbed a tree. There had been no tree in the cage to climb, but somehow she felt sure that she could. She gave a little hop and clung to the trunk with all four feet. Then she reached up and inched a little higher.

But Taffy wanted to play. He seized the middle of her back and pulled her down. She sprawled on the ground, then jumped up and chased him. Then they both chased each other, dodging around and around the tree, first this way and then that. They had never played such a good game before! How could they when they had always lived in that cage?

Soon Taffy ambled off in search of something more to eat. And once again Tansy started up the beech tree. It would have been easier to climb if its trunk had not been so smooth. Her

claws kept slipping and she did not get very high. When she looked down, Taffy was disappearing into the woods.

She slid down backward and ran to catch up. Suddenly she stopped. The boys were in the woods too. She could hear them but could not see them. She flattened herself to the ground behind a thick bush and watched them from behind its leaves.

"It's nice here," said Davy. "*I'd* like to live in the woods."

"You wouldn't really," said Bill.

"Yes, I would," insisted Davy. "Maybe Taffy and Tansy would too. Maybe they'd *rather*."

"Shhhhh," warned Bill. "If they hear us they might hide. They might be right behind those rocks."

Davy ran to look. "I don't see them."

Of course not! Taffy had squeezed himself way back between the rocks until he was pretty well hidden.

When they could no longer hear the boys' voices, Tansy stole from behind the bush and Taffy crept out from among the rocks. The sun was getting low. It shone straight along the ground between the trunks of the trees and lay red on the pine needles. It was the hour when the raccoons had always expected their supper, when they had pressed their faces against

32

the wire of their cage and watched for the boys to come down the path with a pan heaped high with all sorts of good things.

There was no denying that they were very hungry and that all they had found to eat did not begin to fill them up. So when they saw a vine hanging with tight bunches of little, spicy, wild grapes, they ate all they could reach. Nothing had ever tasted half so good.

The sun was gone now and a little cool breeze blew down the brook. The woods were grey. The birds no longer twittered together but were silently finding sleeping places for the night. A chipmunk sat with his head out of his hole taking a last look at the day, and one katydid warned of the coming of the dark.

Taffy and Tansy kept close together. A bat swept over the water and back again hunting mosquitoes. They looked up, then ducked as it flew past their heads with a dull, fluttering sound. They were feeling a little strange without the walls of their cage about them.

"We've got to go home," said Bill. "It's going to be dark pretty soon."

"It's past supper time," said Davy.

They walked down the brook in silence.

34

"Do you think they'll ever come home? Do you, Bill?"

His brother shook his head.

"I liked them. I don't want them to be lost," said Davy unhappily. "Do you think they'll find enough to eat?"

"I guess so," said Bill.

"Do you think anybody will hurt them?"

Bill hesitated. "I hope not," he said.

Suddenly Davy stopped and caught hold of his brother's arm so that he stopped too.

"There's one of them!" he whispered excitedly. "It's Tansy."

"How do you know?" whispered Bill.

"She's got her paws over her eyes. Taffy doesn't do that so much as Tansy. She's sleepy. I *think* that's why she does it."

"Do you suppose we can sneak up on her?" asked Bill softly.

Tansy sat with her head bowed in her arms. Both little hands were clasped tightly over her eyes. But if her eyes were covered, her ears were not! And though the boys thought they were making no noise at all as they crept toward her, she dropped her arms and, lifting her head, looked straight at them.

"Tansy! Tansy!" called Davy softly, coaxingly. "Tansy!"

Tansy stood up and looked at Davy intently. For a moment she hesitated, then, dropping to all fours, turned and ran off.

And suddenly from nowhere Taffy came and ran beside her.

"Hurry!" cried Bill. "Perhaps we can catch them!"

But Tansy ran straight to a big hemlock tree and began to scramble up its rough trunk. She went higher and higher as if she had always climbed trees, and Taffy was climbing right on her heels. By the time the boys reached the foot of the tree, the raccoons were high above their heads.

"Taffy! Tansy!" they both called, but the raccoons only peered down at them curiously and made their way even higher until they were almost hidden among the branches.

"They've got to come down sometime," said Bill. "I'll stay here and watch. You run and tell Mother I've got to wait here until they come down."

"All night?"

"If they don't come down before."

When Davy came back, he carried two blankets.

"Mother says I can stay, too. We're to shout if we want her. She says she could hear us if we both shouted real loud."

It was getting dark. The boys wrapped themselves up in their blankets and settled down on opposite sides of the tree. Now the raccoons could not climb down past them without their knowing. Bill leaned back against the trunk and looked up, but it was too dark to see through the branches.

"Tansy?" called Davy and thought he heard a little answering purr. But she did not come down to have her ears rubbed.

The katydids were beginning to sing, more and more of them as it grew darker. Their scritching filled the familiar woods and made it seem strange and lonely.

"Bill, you're not going to sleep?"

"How can I when those old katydids are making such a noise?"

The night seemed very long. When the first grey light sifted through the hemlock, Bill strained his eyes to look along every limb all the way to the top. The tree was empty.

"Davy, Davy, wake up!"

Davy staggered to his feet. "Are they coming down?"

"They've gone," said Bill.

"How could they?" wailed Davy. "How could they get by us?"

"They didn't. They must have gone through the treetops. I guess they went home."

"To their cage?"

But Bill shook his head and said gruffly,

"To their woods."